SNOW DAY!

Patricia Lakin

pictures by Scott Nash

DIAL BOOKS FOR YOUNG READERS

New York

For Lee, who always valued a snow day with our sons
—P.L.

To Di, Dunc and Frank, with love
—S.N.

Published by Dial Books for Young Readers
A division of Penguin Putnam Inc.
345 Hudson Street
New York, New York 10014
Text copyright © 2002 by Patricia Lakin
Pictures copyright © 2002 by Scott Nash
All rights reserved
Designed by Kimi Weart and Scott Nash
Printed in Hong Kong on acid-free paper

1 3 5 7 9 10 8 6 4 2

Library of Congress Cataloging-in-Publication Data
Lakin, Pat.
Snow day! / Patricia Lakin ; pictures by Scott Nash.
p. cm.
Summary: Four friends enjoy a snowy day of sledding.
ISBN 0-8037-2642-2
[1. Snow—Fiction. 2. Sleds—Fiction.]
I. Nash, Scott, date, ill. II. Title.
PZ7.L1586 Sn 2002
[E]—dc21   00-063874

The illustrations were created using gouache and pencil.

"Look!"

said Sam.

"WHERE?"
said Pam.

"S N

said Sam, Pam,

Will and Jill.

"Long undies," said Sam.

"Boots," said Pam.

"Mittens," said Will.

"Scarves," said Jill.

"S L E

said Sam, Pam,

D S !"

Will and Jill.

"We forgot,"
said Sam.

"What?" said Pam.

"Our helmets," said Will.

"Our goggles," said Jill.

said Sam, Pam, Will and Jill.

"The yard?"
said Sam.

"The walk?"
said Pam.

"The drive?"
said Will.

"The hill?"
said Jill.

"YES!" said Sam, Pam, Will and Jill.

"STOP!" said Sam.
"What for?" said Pam.
"What now?" said Will.
"What's up?" said Jill.

"School," said Sam.

"SCHOOL,"

sighed Sam, Pam, Will and Jill.

"We can fix it," said Sam.
"If we scram," said Pam.
"Let's hurry!" said Will.
"Let's go!" said Jill.

"NOW!"
said Sam, Pam, Will and Jill.

They threw down their sleds.
They ran inside.

They took off their mittens.

They took off their boots.

They took off their goggles.

They took off their helmets.

They took off their scarves.

They ran to their phones.
They phoned in the news.

"This is Principal Sam,"
said Sam.

"This is Principal Pam,"
said Pam.

"This is Principal Will,"
said Will.

"This is Principal Jill,"
said Jill.

"Snow day today!"
they all said.

"All schools are
Sam, Pam,

closed!" said the news.
Will and Jill smiled.

  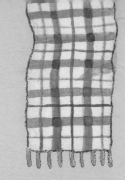 

They put on their scarves.

They put on their helmets.

   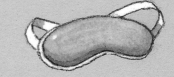

They put on their goggles.

They put on their boots.

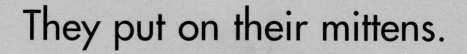

They put on their mittens.

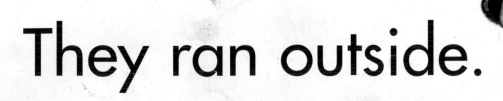

They ran outside.

They picked up their sleds.
They ran up the hill.

"Wheee!"
sang Sam, Pam, Will and Jill.
And they sledded and sledded all day.